Make way for the monsters from
MONSTER MANOR

#1 Von Skalpel's Experiment

#2 Frankie Rocks the House

#3 Beatrice's Spells

#4 Wolf Man Stu Bites Back

Coming soon:

#5 Horror Gets Slimed

MONSTER MANOR
Wolf Man Stu Bites Back

by **PAUL MARTIN** and **MANU BOISTEAU**
Adapted by LISA PAPADEMETRIOU
Illustrated by MANU BOISTEAU

Hyperion Books for Children
New York

First published under the title *Maudit Manoir,*
Bernard le Loup-Garou
in France by Bayard Jeunesse.
© Bayard Editions Jeunesse, 2001
Text Copyright © 2001 by Paul Martin
Illustrations copyright © 2001 by Manu Boisteau
Monster Manor, Volo, and the Volo colophon
are trademarks of Disney Enterprises, Inc.
Volo® is a registered trademark of Disney Enterprises, Inc.

Printed in the United States of America
First U.S. edition, 2004
1 3 5 7 9 10 8 6 4 2
This book is set in 13-point Excelsior.

ISBN 0-7868-1722-4

Visit www.volobooks.com

Contents

1. The Big, Bad Werewolf   1

2. Von Skalpel's Big News   11

3. Worse and Worser   17

4. What's Up, Dawg?   24

5. Fur B Gone   30

6. Stu's Big Plan   37

7. No News Is Good News   46

8. Magic, Schmagic   56

9. Mister Romance   63

10. The Tables Turn   70

If you're ever in Transylvaniaville, be sure to stop by Mon Staire Manor. Everyone calls it *Monster* Manor... that's because a bunch of monsters live there.

The Haunted Hills

Nerdburg

Transylvaniaville

Malibu Nightclub

MALIBU

A Scary-looking Tree

The Slippen Falls

There are lots of fun things to do at the Manor. You can stroll through the cemetery, watch the swamp glow under the moonlight, or make a few new friends!

The FEMUR Family

EYE-GORE & STEVE

This sweet little family may look scary, but the truth is that they have no guts at all.

They want to be skate punks, but they're really just zombies with bad attitudes.

BEATRICE Mon Staire

She's haunted by a horrible secret...and a hairdo that's even worse.

Wolf Man STU

When the moon is full, he becomes human. Well, *somewhat* human...

COUNT SNOBULA

He isn't rich, but he *is* totally stuck up. Thank goodness he sleeps all day.

Step through the gate— let's see who's home!

The SWAMP HORROR

It ain't easy being a big green ball of toxic slime!

SALLY the Specter

Beatrice's mother is smart, sassy—and a ghost!

Professor VON SKALPEL

The most brilliant mad scientist in town. He's a real cutup.

FRANKIE

Created by Von Skalpel,
Frankie is one of a kind.
Thank goodness.

Take a look inside the Manor.
It might be old, but the monsters
think of it as "home, sweet home."

Von Skalpe
Room

The
Secr

Von
Lab

The
Femur Crypt

Eye-Gore
and
Steve's Pit

The Radioactive Swamp

Wolf Man Stu will make you howl!

CHAPTER ONE
The Big, Bad Werewolf

It was a very balmy spring night in Transylvaniaville. But that didn't mean the villagers were outside enjoying themselves. Normally, they would have been going on hayrides, building bonfires, or dancing the night away at the hippest (and only) nightclub in town, the Malibu. But tonight they were all shut up in their homes, with their doors locked and their windows nailed closed. The people of Transylvaniaville were usually pretty nervous,

1

but this was a little extreme.

The fact was, there was a house at the edge of town that was downright creepy. It was named Mon Staire Manor, but everyone called it Monster Manor, because a group of monsters lived there. And lately, there was a rumor that one of the monsters was creeping around at night, letting all of the sheep on nearby farms out of their pens.

Why a monster would want to do that was a mystery. But the townsfolk weren't taking any chances.

That was why there was only one man on the road that night. Ivan Screaming was holding onto the handlebars of his bicycle so hard that his knuckles were white. It was just his luck that tonight he had to go to the one place where any other sane villager would refuse to go. But what could Ivan do? Someone at

Monster Manor had ordered pizza, and Ivan was the delivery boy.

Even monsters need pizza sometimes.

The dark trees cast eerie shadows overhead as Ivan made his way along the dirt road, the wheels of his bicycle creaking. Ivan looked left, then right. The moon wasn't out yet, and in the darkness, every shrub looked terrifying. Suddenly, there was a rustling noise to Ivan's right. His blood ran icy-cold, and he steered his bicycle away, nearly falling over as his pizza bag pitched forward.

Just as he was about to scream, Ivan saw a small squirrel leap out of the bushes. It blinked at him, then leapt back into the forest, its fluffy tail disappearing into the shrubbery.

Ivan was so relieved that he started to laugh. He giggled, then guffawed, looking backward at the place where the big, scary squirrel had jumped out at him.

That was why Ivan didn't see the dark shadow that swung out at him, right into the middle of the road.

"Aaaaaah!" Ivan shouted, as he ran into the creature with his bicycle.

"Ooof!" the creature grunted, as Ivan went flying and then landed several feet away.

Ivan jumped up. "I'm so sorry—" he began, but when he saw the bloodred eyes, white fangs, and coat of fur that covered the creature he had hit, he gulped.

"I'm very hungry," the werewolf said, grinning at the delivery boy. He held a fork in his hand. . . .

COWABUNGA!

Several minutes later, Wolf Man Stu walked into Monster Manor carrying the pizza boxes. The living room was crammed with all of the Manor's residents. As usual, the various creatures were crowded around the television set.

"What took you so long?" asked Eye-Gore, one of the grouchy teenage zombies who lived in the crypts behind the manor.

"Grrr—all of these delivery folks are useless," Wolf Man Stu growled as he plopped the pizza boxes on the dining room table. "This one nearly ran me over!"

Count Snobula, the old vampire, sniffed. "Service has gone down the drain since the seventeen hundreds," he agreed.

Just then, there was a loud squeak. The creatures turned toward the window and watched Ivan wobble away on his bicycle.

"No wonder it took him so long to get here," Steve, the other teenage zombie, said. "His bike is seriously messed up!"

"I jutht hope that my garlic-pepperoni-muthroom-three-thcoopth-of-vanilla-eyeth-cream piztha hathn't melted yet," lisped the little skeleton, Bonehead Femur.

"And I hope that my special tomato sauce is nice and red," Count Snobula put in.

An oozing swamp creature rubbed his huge

belly. (It jiggled like green Jell-O, but wasn't nearly as yummy-looking.) The creature's name was Horror, but he was really a pretty nice guy. "If they overcooked my spinach-and-broccoli pizza," Horror said, "I'll be very upset. Last time, my pizza looked like a puddle of slime!"

Eye-Gore turned to Wolf Man Stu. "Hand over the pizza, dogbreath."

The creatures surrounded Wolf Man Stu, and reached for the stack of boxes he had pulled from the bag. But the minute the monsters touched the pile, it tipped and scattered all over the floor.

"Oh, no!" Horror cried, reaching for the top box. He opened the lid, expecting to find a gooey mess. Instead he found . . .

eedy Pizza sure
t give you much for
money . . . ha-ha!
Burp!
Ha-ha-ha-ha!

"Nothing?" Horror stared at the empty box. "Where's the pizza?"

The other creatures began ripping open the boxes. Bonehead cried when he saw that all that was left of his pizza was a small glob of vanilla ice cream with a tiny piece of pepperoni on top.

"Every single one of these boxes is empty!" cried Beatrice Mon Staire. She was the owner of the Manor and a sort-of witch. That is, she could be kind of witchy, but didn't really know any magic.

Wolf Man Stu grinned and shrugged. "I guess that delivery boy must have given our pizzas to somebody else. . . ."

"Liar!" Beatrice cried, pointing at Wolf Man Stu. "You gobbled up all nine pizzas!"

"That's not true!" Stu insisted.

"Then why is the fur on your chin covered

with tomato sauce and crumbs?" asked Fibula
Femur, the father of the skeleton family.

"You're a thief!" shouted Beatrice's mother,
Sally, the only ghost in the manor. "And a
greedy, greedy hog!"

"You bloodsucker!" Count Snobula cried.
"You're always raiding the refrigerator!"

"Yeah, and he leaves fur on the sofa, which
I have to clean up," Frankie, the manor
handyman said. Of course, Frankie was also
assistant to Professor Von Skalpel, the mad

scientist, so he had many things to clean up that were far worse than a little fur.

"Oh, all right," Wolf Man Stu finally admitted. "I devoured everything. But I'm a werewolf! A vicious creature of the night! I get grumpy if I don't eat—and you don't want to see me grumpy!" Stu bared his fangs.

Horror rolled his eyes. "You're *always* grumpy," he pointed out.

"That's because I'm always hungry!" Wolf Man Stu shouted. "Look, I didn't ask to become a werewolf! Do you think it's fun being covered in itchy fur and fleas? If you don't like it, why don't you talk to—"

At that moment, the door swung open. "Come qvickly, everyvun!" Professor Von Skalpel shouted in his strange accent. "I have somezing to show you!"

CHAPTER TWO

Von Skalpel's Big News

Everyone forgot about the werewolf and the empty pizza boxes and turned to stare at Professor Von Skalpel.

"What's going on?" Frankie asked. The professor had put Frankie together with spare body parts that he had dug up from the local cemetery, near the radioactive swamp. Frankie still thought of the professor as his dad. Kind of.

"It is zee villagers," the professor said

breathlessly. "Zey are furious! All of Transylvaniaville is going on a hunt!" At that moment, the professor saw the empty pizza boxes. "You did not save me any pizza?" he asked, sounding hurt.

"Are there very many villagers?" Kneecap Femur, Bonehead's little sister, asked.

"Zey have gazzered every veapon in zee town. Zey have pitchforks. Zey have torches. Some of zem even have heavy sausages," the professor said. "It seems zey are hunting . . . a monster."

Everyone froze.

"But why?" Radius Femur asked.

"Somevun has been letting zee Transylvaniaville sheep out of zair pens at night," the professor said. "Zey sink zat only a deranged monschter is capable of such a sing. Besides, zey found zome schtrange tracks near zee sheep—zee  tracks of a very large animal. And zee last schtraw came tonight. It seems zat a young pizza delivery boy vas attacked by a hideous monster with horrible breath!"

"Bad breath!" Wolf Man Stu cried.

"Stu, that's it," Beatrice said coldly. "You never pay your rent on time, you gobbled up our pizza, leaving nothing but a blob of ice cream, and now the villagers are going to come to my house and burn the place down! I think I speak for everyone when I tell you to leave quickly, before the villagers get here and whack us on the head with greasy sausages."

"And I'll bet they altho have vithiouth killer dogth," Bonehead put in. "And knivth—"

13

"Okay, baby bones, we get it," Steve said.

"I can't believe you'd turn over one of your own just because a couple of villagers raided their tool sheds and refrigerators," Wolf Man Stu shouted.

"You aren't one of us!" Count Snobula yelled. "You came here by accident and you stayed out of laziness. And now you've gone on this insane sheep crusade!"

"I never did anything to any sheep!" Stu insisted. "Why would I? I don't even like sheep."

"You eat pigeons," Horror pointed out. "And once you gobbled up the mailman."

"Pigeons are tasty!" Stu said.

"Tell zat to zee villagers who are marching up zee road to zee Manor!" Professor Von Skalpel cried. "Frankie, toss him outside!"

Frankie got up and grabbed the werewolf by the scruff of the neck.

"Grrr!" Stu growled. "Put me down! I'm a ferocious beast! I'll tear you limb from limb!"

Frankie just sighed and carried Stu out the front door. All of the other monsters followed as Frankie chucked Stu onto the road, slamming the iron fence behind him. Beatrice took out an old iron key and double-locked the bolt. Then she taped a note to the fence:

Dear Villagers,

The monster you are after has been tossed out of the Manor. Please go away, and try to cause as little damage as possible.

Yours truly,

Beatrice Mon Staire

P.S.: Feel free to leave the sausages. We're starving.

Stu read the note and growled as the creatures retreated toward the Manor. "Grrr . . . I'll be back!" he cried. "You'll regret treating me like a dog!"

But the only response was the faint sound of Frankie's voice from the living room. "Come quick, everyone! The show's about to start!"

The monsters hurried back into the house.

"Fine!" Wolf Man Stu shouted. "Good-bye! I get no respect around here, anyway." Laughter trickled out of the Manor's windows as the monsters giggled at something on TV. "Go on, laugh!" Stu shouted as he kicked at the gate. "My life can't possibly get any worse!"

CHAPTER THREE
Worse and Worser

Just then, lightning cracked across the sky, and it began to rain.

"Okay, so my life *can* get worse," Stu grumbled, as he ducked under a tree. Ugh. He was already starting to smell like wet dog. Wolf Man Stu let out a low growl and began to make a mental to-do list:

1. Get revenge on monsters that kicked me out of the Manor.

2. Avoid villagers armed with heavy

sausages and pitchforks.

3. Solve the sheep mystery.

What is the deal with the sheep, anyway? the wolf man wondered.

It was a fact known around the world that the Transylvaniaville sheep were amazingly fluffy. The villagers made soft sweaters and blankets with the wool. Without the money from the Transylvaniaville "no-itch" sheep, half of the village would have gone broke.

Wolf Man Stu coughed slightly as he headed up the road toward the nearest farm. I can hardly see where I'm going, he thought, feeling sorry for himself. It's so dark out.

It was *very* dark out, because the moon was hidden behind big, black, rain clouds. This weather is giving me the sniffles, Wolf Man Stu thought miserably as he reached the farm.

I can hardly smell anything. Even though his nose was stuffy, he could still smell the stink of the wet sheep. He caught a whiff of wood smoke and then—*achoo!*—the smell of feathers.

Perfect, the wolf man thought. He was allergic to feathers.

But he still didn't smell what he was sniffing for—the monster who had been setting free all the sheep.

Okay, here's the plan, Wolf Man Stu told himself as he crept toward the sheep pen. I'll hide among the sheep until the criminal shows up. Then I'll make a citizen's arrest. Simple.

But when Stu tried to get near the sheep, they just bleated and ran away. "Come back!" Stu growled, but the sheep just kept running in circles. Ugh, Stu thought, no wonder I hate sheep.

All right, Stu said to himself, maybe it's time for Plan B.

Just then, Stu's sensitive hearing picked up the sound of the approaching mob.

"Death to the sheep thief!" someone cried.

"Whack him with a sausage!" someone else shouted.

"Look!" a third voice said. "Claw prints— near the sheep pen!"

Stu darted behind a large tree. He could see

the light
from the
torches
heading
toward him.
There had to be
more than a hundred
villagers in the crowd.
Some of them had large,
ferocious dogs. Others
had ferocious miniature poodles. And the villagers did seem to
have every available weapon in the town. One
woman even carried a head of lettuce.

What should I do? Stu wondered as he
stared at the mob. Quickly, he hopped into a
nearby stream to hide while he thought.

Stu decided to do what he usually did when
he was in trouble—hide in a tree.

In a flash, he had scrambled out of the creek and up a large, old tree nearby. He barely made it in time. The villagers arrived just as he got settled among the top branches.

"Do you smell anything, boy?" one of the villagers asked his poodle.

The dog yapped once, then twice. Stu held his breath.

"He says no!" the villager shouted.

"Don't talk crazy!" another villager called. "Poodles are from France—they don't speak English!"

"This one is bilingual!" the first villager shouted back. "Come on! The monster must have gone downriver."

Stu blinked in surprise as the villagers continued on. I guess the poodle didn't know I was here, because I just smell like wet dog, he figured. Finally—my luck is improving!

Just then, a feather tickled his nose. Stu looked after the villagers. They weren't that far away yet. He tried to hold back, but he couldn't help it. . . .

Achoo!

Stu let out a sneeze that was about as loud as the space shuttle taking off. At that moment, the full moon came out from behind a cloud and lit up the forest.

Below him, a nervous voice called, "Who was that?"

CHAPTER FOUR
What's Up, Dawg?

Stu pressed himself against the tree, but it was no use.

"Hey, you!" shouted a nasal voice. "What are you doing up in that tree?" It was a woman's voice. "Come down right now!" she commanded.

I can't let her keep shouting, Wolf Man Stu thought, or the villagers will come back! He scrambled down the tree, which seemed to have unusually rough bark. Maybe she'll think

I'm a poodle, Stu thought hopefully.

When the woman saw him, her eyes grew round. "Oh, my! Your hands are bleeding!" she said.

"Woof!" Wolf Man Stu said, doing his best dog impersonation. "Woof! Woo—what?"

The woman was looking at him strangely. She had red hair and a big smile.

Stu had just realized that she had said, "hands," not "claws." Looking down, he saw that he did, in fact, have two human hands. And that his skin was badly scratched from climbing down the tree just then.

Stu nearly used one of his hands to smack himself in the forehead. Of course! The full moon! He'd been so freaked out by the mob of angry villagers that he'd forgotten about it.

Usually, werewolves spent most of their time as humans and became animals only under the light of the full moon. But for Stu, it was the opposite. He looked like a wolf most of the time, and only became a man when the moon was full. Tonight, he'd been tossed out of the Manor before he had had time to check his calendar.

"Let me see your hands," the woman said, walking toward him. "Why were you up in that tree?" she asked. She fished in her pants pocket and came up with a Band-Aid.

"Uh . . . I thought it might be a good idea to

take a look up above," Stu lied. "You know, in case the beast can fly."

"You think it can fly?" the woman asked nervously. "What makes you think that? You didn't . . . see anything suspicious up there, did you?"

"Oh, no," Stu said quickly. "But you can never be too careful."

The woman narrowed her eyes. "I don't think I've seen you around Transylvaniaville," she said slowly. "I just moved here. My name is Fiona, but my friends call me Daisy."

"My name is Wolf—" Stu caught himself just in time. "Wolf*gang* Stuart," he said. "Of the Nerdberg Stuarts. Nice to meet you."

"What do you do?" Daisy asked.

"Well, I used to be a cosmetics salesman," Stu said. "I travel around a lot," he went on. "I'm kind of a lone wolf."

"I know what you mean, Wolfgang," Daisy said with a sigh.

"Call me Stu. All my friends do."

Daisy smiled. "I know what you mean, *Stu*," she corrected herself. "That's why I moved to the country." She finished bandaging his hand. "There," she said. "Good as new."

Stu glanced at the sky. He knew he had to be careful—if the moon went behind a cloud again, he'd go back to being a werewolf. The villagers still weren't all that far away. I have to get out of here, Stu thought.

"You know, my hands are really killing me," Stu explained. "I think I'm just going to go home. You'd better hurry or you won't be able to catch up to the others!"

"Won't you walk with me—at least

part of the way?" Daisy asked. "I don't feel safe with a beast roaming around!"

"Really, I can't," Stu said.

Daisy sighed again.

Actually, Stu felt kind of bad for leaving Daisy behind. After all, no one at Monster Manor had treated him that well in a long time. "But maybe I'll see you around," Stu added quickly. "Thanks again for bandaging my paw—er—hand. Bye!'"

Stu turned and scurried away from Daisy. Finally, he came to the path he was looking for. He'd just had a great idea about where he could spend the night. . . .

CHAPTER FIVE
Fur B Gone

Stu was still human, but he looked absolutely beastly. His old T-shirt was torn and covered in leaves and tree bark, and his pants were muddy and ripped. To top it off, he smelled like wet dog. But Stu didn't let any of that get him down. He had a plan that couldn't fail.

Stu followed the narrow path, and eventually came out of the woods. He grinned. He was only a few hundred yards from the manor.

A moment later, he came to a clearing where the full moon shone down on a rusted car. Stu shook his head and sighed. This old Chevy was the only link to his past—his glamorous former life as a door-to-door makeup salesman.

It had been seven long years since he had driven this very car into Transylvaniaville.

Back then, Stu hadn't been a werewolf. No, he had been Stuart Lourdel, top-ranked Jenny G Cosmetics salesman for the entire northeast region. He had loved selling makeup. He made good money and he beautified the environment. What was not to love?

But then he had called on Monster Manor. A few guys down at the local bar had warned Stu that Monster Manor was haunted and told him not to go there. They had mentioned Beatrice Mon Staire, and how she could have been good-looking if she hadn't had such a

horrible hairdo and if she had maybe smiled
once in a while. Stu had decided that Beatrice
Mon Staire sounded like a lady who needed
some beauty products. Hair gel could work
wonders for an awful 'do. And maybe some
nice, relaxing bath salts would put a smile on
her face!

Stu had headed for the Manor with a sample bag full of cosmetics. He was so excited
that he'd even sung along with the radio as he

drove. But when Stu had rung the Manor's bell, it hadn't been Beatrice who answered the door—it had been a short, balding man in dark glasses.

What an idiot I was, Stu thought now, remembering.

Stu had assumed that Professor Von Skalpel was Beatrice's husband, and he had immediately tried to sell him some cosmetics. The mad scientist had been delighted, and had offered Stu a stick of chewing gum. Of course, there was no way that Stu could have known not to accept a stick of chewing gum from Professor Von Skalpel. The professor claimed that he was trying to create a special flavor, but when Stu popped the gum in his mouth, he immediately turned into a furry, smelly monster with fleas.

"Sorry!" the professor had said. "I don't

know how to turn you back into a man. Vhoopsie!"

But now, all these years later, Stu finally had an idea.

Stu popped the trunk of his car. Amazingly, his things were still there! He pulled out his old case of beauty products and a spare set of clothes that he had wrapped in plastic. Stu used some toner to cleanse his face, then rubbed his scratched hands with some nice-smelling antibacterial moisturizer. By the time the moon set, Stu had turned back into a werewolf—but he was a much cleaner and less stinky werewolf than he had been before.

Actually, Stu told him-

self as he stepped into his old suit, *I'm looking pretty sharp.*

The wolf man pulled out a tube of Hair B Gone, and rubbed it over his hands. As he did, he hummed the Hair B Gone jingle to himself:

Who wants to shave—
It's a bother and a bore!
Legs, face, or armpits,
It's an awful chore!
But Hair B Gone will fix ya,
All your friends will say, "Hey—whoa!"
'Cause your hair will fall out and it won't
*   come back.*
Hair B Gone! When you want the hair
*   to go!*

Stu laughed as he sang, and made up his own line: "Hey there, werewolves, it's also good for you! Hair B Gone gets rid of fur, too!"

Stu didn't have enough Hair B Gone for his whole body, so he decided to focus on his hands and feet. His skin was kind of grayish and rough, so he slathered on a thick layer of Think Pink! pig's-milk lotion. That made his hands and feet a little pinker and smoother. Then he used a nail clipper and file to tame his claws. Without all of that fur on his feet, he even managed to slip on his shoes!

Stu stashed his cosmetics in a paper bag and walked toward the Manor with a bounce in his step. I am looking good! he thought. And now for Phase Two of my brilliant plan!

Stu was only a few steps away from the Manor when he caught sight of his own reflection in one of the windows.

Oh, my gosh! Stu thought, horrified. I forgot about my head!

CHAPTER SIX
Stu's Big Plan

Professor Von Scalpel hurried from the front door to the Manor gate. Who was that elegant stranger who had just rung the bell? His suit, tie, and shiny shoes made him look like someone from the city. And yet there was something unusual about this man—something unique and different. Perhaps it was the paper bag he was wearing on his head. . . .

"Vhat can I do for you?" the professor asked from behind the gate.

"Hello," the mysterious stranger said in a charming voice, "are you Herman Von Skalpel, the mad—er—*famous* scientist?"

"Vhy, yes," the professor said, flattered. "How can I help you?"

"My name is . . . uh . . . Wolfgang Stuart," the man with the bag on his head went on.

(Okay, for those of you who haven't figured it out yet, the guy with the bag on his head is really Stu. But don't tell the professor! It's all part of the plan.)

"The University of Nerdberg has sent me here to take a look at your work," Stu told the professor. "As you may know, we have a special prize for research in the area of chewing gum."

Professor Von Skalpel's heart beat a little faster. Could it be true? Could the University of Nerdberg really have sent someone here to award him the famous I. B. Chompin Chewing Gum Prize?

Zis is zee answer to all of my prayers! Von Skalpel thought happily.

"Professor!" someone shouted. "Is this man bothering you?"

The professor and "Wolfgang" turned to see Frankie hurrying toward them. He had just been watering the man-eating plants at the side of the house.

"Ah!" Stu said quickly to Professor Von

Skalpel. "I heard that your hobby was putting together monsters made from body parts dug from the cemetery near the radioactive swamp. This must be one of them. How charming!"

Von Skalpel couldn't believe how much the university knew about him! "Don't vorry, Frankie," he said. "Volfgang is a friend."

Stu followed the professor into the kitchen, where the scientist offered him a soda. Stu declined. The last time he had taken something from the professor, he had turned into a wolf. Besides, in order to drink it, I would have to take the paper bag off my head, Stu thought. But I am kinda thirsty.

"Forgive me for asking," the professor said, "but vould you mind telling me vhy you are vearing a paper bag on your head?"

"Uh—what bag?" Stu asked nervously.

The professor coughed slightly. Clearly, zis paper-bag man is a little crazy, he thought. Which was okay.

Crazy was something the professor understood. "Um . . . never mind," the professor said. "Vould you like to see my collection of mutant slugs?" Von Skalpel added quickly, changing the subject.

"Absolutely," Stu said. He followed the professor to his laboratory and looked around. "These are beautiful!" Stu said, gazing admiringly, through the holes in his bag, at the slugs that were carefully preserved in glass jars.

"I collected zem all in zee radioactive svamp," the professor said proudly.

Stu let the professor show him all around

the lab. Stu was sure to ooh and aah over everything. "You know, the university is interested in another of your side studies," he said finally. "Man-to-beast transformation."

Professor Von Skalpel scratched his head. "Do you mean my verevolf chewving gum?" he asked. "I only did zat vunce—and it vas by mistake. I dipped it into a cup of tea zat Beatrice had infused viz a schpell. Schtrangely, no vun vanted to try my chewving gum after zat." The professor rubbed his chin and looked thoughtful.

"You mean that you never came up with an antidote?" Stu demanded, his voice rising. "Never?"

"Vhat?" the professor asked, frowning.

"Don't you have something that can undo what you did to me?" Stu cried. He lunged at the professor. "Give me anything!"

Von Skalpel was crazy, but he wasn't stupid. It only took him a moment to realize that the man beneath the bag was Wolf Man Stu! The professor hardly had enough time to wonder how the wolf man had made his hands so pink and silky-smooth before he sprang away. "Aaargh!" he cried. "Don't bite me!"

"Do you have an antidote or don't you?" Stu hollered, as he continued to chase the professor around the lab.

"Of course I do!" the professor lied. "It's

called . . . uh . . . Volf No More." He ducked beneath a table and skittered to the other side of the lab. "It also gets rid of fleas."

"Give it to me," Stu growled.

"Um . . . sorry, I don't have any left," the professor said quickly. "I sold all of it to a pharmacy in Nerdberg five years ago in order to pay for my chewving gum research."

"Do they have any left?" Stu asked.

"Probably," the professor said with a shrug. "Zere is not a big demand for zee schtuff."

"Which pharmacy did you sell it to?" Stu demanded. "There must be a hundred pharmacies in Nerdberg."

"I don't remember," the professor said. "But I could make you a small batch of zee schtuff—it vill only take me about two montz. Perhaps you could have it in time to attend zee avard ceremony for my chewving gum research. . . ."

"Birdbrain!" Wolf Man Stu shouted. "You're not getting any award! And you'll never see me again!"

With that, the werewolf jumped out the window and headed toward Nerdberg. Von Skalpel watched him go and heaved a sigh of relief.

Poor volf, he said to himself. I never made an antidote. But hopefully he vill have calmed down by zee time he has checked every pharmacy in Nerdberg. At least it vill be qviet around here . . . for a little vhile.

CHAPTER SEVEN
No News Is Good News

*T*hree weeks passed with the flip of a page.

Daisy sat tucked into her armchair, watching the *Nerdberg News at Eleven*. The anchorman, Brad Guy, frowned seriously as he read the latest news off the TelePrompTer.

"Two more herds of sheep have been set free and were found wandering the hills near Transylvaniaville," Brad Guy said. "The villagers have been living a nightmare for the last month, where some sort of deranged beast has gone on a sheep-freedom crusade. Some Transylvaniavillians suspect that the beast has a high I.Q., as it has managed to outsmart all of their traps so far. . . ."

The scene changed to show a big hole in the ground. "We dug this pit near the sheep," explained a woman from Transylvaniaville. "And the monster didn't even fall into it!"

"Maybe next time we'll have to cover it with leaves, or something," her husband added.

The woman, Daisy, sighed. "This can't go on," she muttered. "I have to do something—but I don't have much time. I have to find Wolfgang Stuart. But I haven't seen him since the night we met. . . ." She shook her head, trying to think. Come on, Daisy, she told herself. Straighten up and fly right! You have to come up with a plan. . . .

Daisy pulled herself out of her chair and

snapped off the TV just as Brad Guy finished his report on Transylvaniaville. "And in completely unrelated news," Brad Guy went on, "In Nerdberg, the drugstore bandit strikes again—"

Meanwhile, back at the Manor, everyone was huddled around the TV watching the news. Everyone except Wolf Man Stu, of course.

"Residents of Nerdberg are concerned about this recent bunch of drugstore burglaries," Brad Guy droned from the TV. "Here is an eyewitness account from U. R. Illin, the pharmacist at Sneezemore's Drugs."

A pudgy man with thick glasses flashed onto the screen. "It was five minutes to eight, and I was about to close up, when a man walked into the store. There was something strange about him—maybe it was his nice suit.

Or maybe it was the paper bag over his head. Anyway, I thought to myself, Self, this guy probably has a pimple problem. So I suggested GreatFace, a cream with an oyster-liver base. It smells horrible, but it works. The paper-bag guy told me that he only used Jenny G cosmetics. Then he told me that he wanted my entire stock of Wolf No More. When I told him I'd never heard of it, he went nuts and shoved all of my breath mints off the shelf! Then he stormed out!"

Horror and Eye-Gore the zombie cracked up.

"Professor," Count Snobula asked, "are you sure Wolf Man Stu is the drugstore bandit?" The vampire frowned. "It doesn't seem like him to attack a bunch of breath mints that way. . . ."

"It is definitely Schtu," Von Skalpel said. "Vhy else vould zee drugstore bandit ask for Volf No More, when zee schtuff does not even really exist? Besides, I told you all about how he came here viz a paper bag on his head. . . ."

"Unfortunately, Professor," Beatrice said, "I don't think that we have much time left before Stu comes back—in a worse mood than when he left."

"What do you mean?" Frankie asked.

"Stu has attacked twenty-seven drugstores in the past three weeks," Beatrice explained. Then she held up a thick, yellow book. "As you

can see from the Yellow Pages, there are only twenty-eight pharmacies in Nerdberg." She slammed the phone book down on the table.

Everyone froze.

"Really?" the professor asked. "I zought zere vere more like a hundred."

"So you think Stu will come back soon?" Fibula Femur asked.

"And that he'll be very grumpy when he

does?" his wife, Tibia, added.

"Oh, I'm sure he vill have calmed down by zee time he comes back," Von Skalpel suggested in a trembling voice.

"Hmm," Beatrice said. "Well, Stu was never really known for being calm. I guess I'll just start locking myself in my bedroom every night. Speaking of which, good night!" Beatrice waved cheerfully as she left the room. "And pleasant dreams, everyone!"

For a moment, the room was silent except for the drone of the television set. Finally, Fibula looked at the clock on the wall. "All right, children," he said quickly, "it's getting late. We'd better get back to the cemetery!"

"Uh, yeah," Steve the zombie agreed. "Eye-Gore and I will go with you."

"Me, too," Horror added quickly.

The living room was empty in a matter of

moments. Frankie was the last to leave. He didn't like to watch TV by himself. He yawned and walked over to the television set.

Frankie was tired after spending all day trying to tame the biting weeds in the backyard. One of them had even bitten him on the finger. Maybe that was why he didn't pay attention when Brad Guy said, "This just in—another pharmacy in Nerdberg was attacked less than an hour ago. That makes twenty-eight pharmacies in less than twenty-one days—"

Beatrice walked into her room and frowned. What is going on? she wondered. Her room looked as though it had been hit by a tornado. Suddenly, Beatrice felt a cold chill. That was when she noticed that the window was wide open. Her carpet was soaked with rain.

"I can't believe I left this open," Beatrice

said as she shut the window. Just as she went to close the drapes, she noticed an unfamiliar and unpleasant smell—a little like wet dog. Just then, Stu leapt out from behind the door and growled. He covered Beatrice's mouth with a pink, manicured hand.

"Don't scream!" he warned her. "I don't

want to hurt you. Well, you did throw me out of the Manor, so I kind of want to hurt you—but I won't, just to show you what a nice guy I am. Von Skalpel lied to me, and now the only person who can help me is you. I need your magical powers."

Beatrice could have told Stu that she was probably as good at magic as the Swamp Horror was at belly dancing, but she didn't. For one thing, Stu still had his hand over her mouth. For another, she didn't want him to trash her the way he had trashed the breath mints in the pharmacy. So Beatrice just pointed to the large bookcases that lined an entire wall of her bedroom.

"Great idea!" Stu growled, a grin spreading across his face. "You've got to have a spell in one of those books. We'll take a look at them together and then I'll get out of here."

CHAPTER EIGHT
Magic, Schmagic

Beatrice's relatives had taken many years to gather the hundreds of books that lined her shelves. Her collection included almost every magic spell in the world. Not that she could do any of them. Beatrice was downright lousy at magic. She couldn't even make the dust bunnies disappear from beneath her bed. She couldn't get rid of the thing with the blue tentacles that lived there, either.

Stu pulled a book from the shelf. "*Spells*

for Fun and Profit," he read. He peered at the spines of some of the other books. "*Magic in Color, Dr. Weevil's Book of Spells* . . . I'm sure we can find what I need in one of these!"

Beatrice shrugged and pulled a book from the top shelf. It was a fat guide to the monsters of the world. She was sure that the answer to Stu's problem was in that book—unfortunately, the book was written in Greek. This is what I hate about magic, Beatrice thought as she flipped through the book. It's so confusing!

Sighing, Beatrice put the book back on her shelf. All these books are confusing, she thought, as she scanned the shelves. Suddenly, her eye fell on a hardcover with a pretty dust jacket. Beatrice slid the book from the shelf and peered at the title: *The Mini-Magician.* It was a children's book, for witches age six and up. Beatrice had bought it in the Transylvaniaville market, and it was the only book in her entire collection that she had actually read from cover to cover. She flipped to the letter W. "Here's some information on werewolves," she said absently.

"Zoinks!" Stu yanked the book from her hand and jumped out the window. "Oof!" he yelled, as he hit the ground.

Beatrice winced. Her bedroom was on the top floor. "What is that crazy werewolf thinking?" she wondered aloud as she slammed shut the window. "Oh, well. At least he's not getting back in this way." Beatrice flipped the lock. "Too bad he took my favorite book."

Stu settled into the front seat of his rusty old Chevy and sifted through the pages until he came to the section on werewolves. He could actually read fairly easily—the storm had blown over and the moon was almost full.

"'A *were* is any creature that is part beast,'" Stu read. "'Usually, but not always, a were is a man who turns into an animal on the night of a full moon. For example, in Britain, there was Joseph the Goff, a sailor who was a man at night and a bear during the day. This made it very difficult for him to get hired by either ships or circuses. Also, not all weres are wolves. There are werefoxes, werepanthers,

even wereanteaters. They're all known for their bad tempers and big appetites. The case of Frederick Roofer, who turned into a kitchen table after a carpentry accident under the light of the full moon, is the only known example of werefurniture.'"

Stu let out a low growl. Had he really jumped out a window for this? This was baby stuff—he already knew most of it! Well, he hadn't known about the werefurniture. Then again, he didn't really care. He scanned the page and finally came to a section on cures.

"How to get rid of a were: Monster hunters

know that only a silver bullet can kill a were. But often weres don't choose to be monsters. Most are victims of a curse or a black-magic accident, such as drinking the wrong potion or accepting a piece of chewing gum from a mad scientist. Many would prefer not to be beasts. Unfortunately, there is only one way to undo the magic—and it isn't easy. The were must make someone fall in love with him. If the were kisses a human under a full moon, he will pass his curse on and be rid of it forever."

Stu snapped the book closed, grinning. Now he had a simple, cheap, painless solution. He felt bad, thinking of the woman who'd be stuck in his smelly wolf skin for the rest of her life. Then again, he'd suffered enough. Let someone else be a beast for a while.

Now all I have to do is find someone and make her fall in love with me before the next full moon! Stu thought as he lay down across the front seat. But who? Beatrice would never fall for a scam like this one, and her mother, Sally, was a ghost. I'm not sure this would work with a ghost, Stu reasoned. Tibia Femur was happily married . . . besides, she was a skeleton. I don't know what a werewolf skeleton would look like, Stu thought, and I'm not sure I want to find out.

No—he'd never be able to make someone at the Manor fall in love with him. He would have to find a stranger. . . .

Wait a minute, Stu thought as he sat up straight. What about that woman who helped me that night I was up in the tree? Yeah, she was nice. And she seemed to like me.

What was her name again?

I've got to g in shape for date! And I n a haircut, tc

CHAPTER NINE
Mister Romance

Daisy's feathers were ruffled. She hadn't been invited out dancing in more than six years! But when she had come home the day before, she had found a romantic letter in her mailbox:

Dear Fiona (or shall I say "Daisy?"),

Do you remember the moonlit night we met by the old oak tree? You treated my wounds—but you didn't know that you had given me a bigger pain . . . in my heart.

I can't stop thinking about you! If you have been thinking about me, too, meet me at the Malibu nightclub at 8 P.M. for dinner and dancing. I'll wait there for you, full of hope!

Yours,

Wolfgang Stuart

P.S.: I have a special surprise for you!

P.P.S.: Enclosed, please find a sample of Stink-Away, Jenny G's finest mouthwash. Also find one of Grease-Off, a conditioner that's perfect for limp, oily hair like yours. Try them! If you like them, I can get you more at a twenty percent discount!

Just thinking about that romantic letter made Daisy's heart skip a beat. Outside, the stars twinkled and the moon was full. Everything was perfect! Daisy glanced at her clock—it was seven-fifteen already! She ripped her best dress from its hanger and stepped into it, glad that it still fit. She hadn't worn it in years.

I hope he thinks I'm pretty, Daisy thought as she brushed her hair. She smiled. The Grease-Off had really worked wonders. "Tonight's the night," she murmured, as she picked up her purse and checked her lipstick.

Just before Daisy left, she glanced at a shabby book that she had carried with her for the past six months. The title was *The Mini-Magician*. And the part she read was about how to get rid of a were.

Daisy arrived at the Malibu at exactly eight o'clock. The Transylvaniaville nightclub was lit up with pink neon, and several hip villagers were already lined up to buy tickets.

Daisy looked around for Stu. She didn't see

him. I hope he doesn't stand me up, Daisy thought, feeling slightly ill.

Achoo!

Daisy turned around and spotted someone behind a nearby trash can. The garbage rattled as the person sneezed again. When the person motioned for her to come over, Daisy finally realized that the sneezing weirdo behind the trash was actually her date.

Slowly, she walked over to join him.

"Sorry," Stu said after he sneezed again. "It's just my allergies. There must be some feathers in this trash. . . ."

"Hmm . . ." Daisy said. "Yeah, about that—why are you hanging around the garbage?"

Of course, Stu could have told Daisy the truth—that he didn't have a dime to his name and couldn't afford the five-dollar charge to get in. But somehow that just didn't seem very classy. Instead, he said, "Oh, this is the VIP entrance. The owner is a buddy of mine—he said that you and I could skip the line. Right this way!"

Stu helped Daisy step onto the top of a couple of garbage cans. "Just haul yourself up through the window," Stu explained.

Once they were through the small window at the back of the club, Stu and Daisy dropped to the floor. For a moment, Stu was sure they would get caught. But everyone was far too busy dancing to Frankie's latest hit, "Jam on the Roll—with Butta," to notice two middle-aged people sneaking into the nightclub.

For Daisy, the night passed like a dream. She and Stu danced nonstop for hours. Stu was pretty good, too—he could kick it like a wild man. Daisy just stuck to her favorite move . . . the funky chicken.

Stu grinned. He hadn't had this much fun in years. In fact, the only time he felt bad was when he remembered his evil plan—to get rid of his curse by passing it on to Daisy. Poor thing, Stu thought with a heavy sigh. Then again, he thought as the next song came on, lucky me!

Only the cool people go through the window!

"Oh, gosh!" Daisy said suddenly, "Do you realize what time it is?"

Stu glanced at the tacky wall clock shaped like a soda can. It was almost four in the morning! His mouth felt dry. Oh no! The moon would set in a few minutes, and then he would turn back into a monster. He had to pass on his curse—now!

Stu leaned forward to kiss Daisy, then hesitated. Could he really do this to her after she'd been so nice to him?

"Let's get out of here," Daisy said suddenly. She grabbed Stu's hand and pulled him toward the door with surprising strength. He could feel the fur beginning to sprout beneath his suit. A chill ran through his body.

That was why he didn't notice that Daisy's hand was clammy, or that it was as cold as ice . . . and slightly webbed. . . .

CHAPTER TEN
The Tables Turn

The moon was beginning to set, and only faint stars lit the village street. Stu breathed a sigh of relief. It was still dark enough so that Daisy couldn't see him changing into a werewolf. He pulled her into the shadow of a nearby tree.

"I guess I should be going," Daisy said. She sounded really disappointed.

All I have to do is kiss her, Stu thought. "Don't leave yet," he begged.

Stu could feel his fangs and claws growing.

His ears were becoming pointy and hair was beginning to sprout from them! I have to act fast, he thought, and pulled Daisy into a hug. Then he leaned in close and got ready to kiss her on the beak. . . .

"Beak?" Stu shouted. He dragged Daisy into the light so he could see her. "Oh, my gosh!" he cried. "You're a—"

"That's right, I'm a duck," the giant bird with Daisy's voice replied. "So now you know my secret." The corners of her beak seemed to curl into a smile and her eyes narrowed as she peered at Stu, who was still hidden in the shadow of a tree. "I'm a wereduck," she went on. "But not for long! All it takes is one little kiss. . . ." She did her best to pucker up.

"Forget it, birdbrain!" Stu cried, as he leapt into the light. "You're not the only one with a curse around here—although I bet you wish you were. Get it? Wish you *were*?" He laughed a little at his own joke.

"A werewolf!" Daisy cried, finally seeing Wolf Man Stu in the light. "Wait a minute. Then, if we kiss . . . I'll become a wolf, and you'll become a giant duck!"

"That's right," Stu said, folding his arms across his chest.

Daisy hesitated a moment, then flapped her wings and flew face to face against Stu. "Even better!" she cried.

"What?" Stu asked, backing away.

"Do you know how lame it is to be a giant duck?" Daisy demanded. "Nobody takes you seriously! At least wolves are scary. And it will be so much easier to continue my animal rights work when I can run around, instead of waddling everywhere."

"Animal rights?" Stu repeated. What is this

crazy bird talking about? he thought.

"Yeah." Daisy thrust her wing into the air. "Power to the nonpeople!" she cried. "We animals have to stick together. That's why I've been setting loose all of the sheep in the area. They should be free, not penned up like prisoners!" Daisy puckered up again and tried to give Stu a kiss on the snout.

Stu dodged away and covered his nose with his paws. But the giant duck swooped toward him again.

"Ugh!" Stu shouted as he darted away. There was no way he was going to let her change him into a duck. I don't get any respect *now*, he thought, and I'm a wild beast of the night. If I become a duck, I'll be the laughing-stock of Transylvaniaville! He staggered away, then ran down the street.

"Just a little kiss!" Daisy quacked as she waddled after him. "Just one!"

"No!" Stu shouted. He poured on the speed as he ran down the road. He had to get help!

Wolf Man Stu was exhausted and out of breath by the time he reached the gate to the Manor. "Open up!" he shouted as he banged on the gate. "I'm being chased by a duck!"

The Manor's front door opened a crack.

"Vhat?" shouted a voice.

"A wereduck is after me!" Stu screamed. "Help me, Professor! She's on an insane sheep-freedom crusade and now she wants to get me!"

Quack! Quack! Daisy was headed up the road.

"Vhat zee heck is zat?" the professor cried as he stumbled into the yard, staring at the giant duck waddling toward the house. Quickly, he swung open the gate and hustled Stu inside. The professor slammed it back into place just in time. Daisy let out a huge quack as the gate slammed shut on her beak.

"Are you all right, professor?" Frankie shouted as he stumbled out of the Manor. "I heard shouting. . . ."

"Go and capture zat sing, Frankie!" Von Skalpel yelled, pointing to the giant duck.

Frankie scrambled over the gate with the

speed and grace of a hippopotamus. Daisy, whose beak was still caught in the gate, had nowhere to run. Frankie caught her easily.

"What's going on here?" Beatrice demanded as she strode out of the Manor. The rest of the monsters were right behind her. "What's all this noise?"

"Someone's been duck hunting," Horror said.

"Ooh, we'll have roast duck tonight. . . . nice and rare," Count Snobula added. He smiled, revealing his sharp front fangs.

Daisy swallowed hard.

"No," Stu said as he stepped forward. "Wait." He looked from the monsters to Daisy. "This duck may be crazy, but she's really a very nice person," he said.

Daisy let out a small quack.

"Besides," Stu went on, "she's the only

proof of my innocence. We have to tell the villagers that *she's* the one who has been setting free the sheep."

"This is the monster that has been outsmarting the villagers for weeks?" Beatrice asked. "Hmm . . . she must be brighter than she looks."

"Enough!" Professor Von Skalpel said. "Frankie, bring me some rope and a vheelbarrow right avay."

Frankie ran to the lab, then helped the professor tie up the duck. They hauled Daisy into the wheelbarrow, and the professor wheeled her into town. It was still early in the morning, so most of the villagers were

Don't worry.

The professor is a nice guy!

Bye, duck.

asleep. The professor steered Daisy to the park in the center of town. Then Beatrice taped a sign to Daisy that read:

Dear Villagers:

Here is the monster who has been freeing your sheep. She has never lived at Mon Staire Manor and never will. Please do not set the poodles on her, as she is really a very nice person and thought she was doing the right thing.

Yours truly,

Beatrice Mon Staire

When the villagers found Daisy, they didn't beat her with a sausage or turn their vicious dogs on her. Instead, they forced her to help them gather their sheep, then made her live at the zoo. Daisy didn't really mind. It turned out that there were a lot of other wereducks at the local zoo. Some of them had even formed a book club, and they let Daisy join. She was happier than she had been in years. And the villagers were happy, too. Not only did the village make money from their sweater sales that year, they had a new attraction for tourists—a huge, talking duck.

As for Stu, he went back to living at the Manor. The other creatures made him promise not to gobble up all of the pizza or scare the delivery boy ever again. Stu swore an oath, and even kept his promise . . . for a whole week.

Stu even decided that he really didn't mind being a werewolf that much. The truth was, being a cosmetics salesman had been glamorous—but it could also get lonely.

"Move over, *Block*head," Stu snarled as he settled onto the couch next to Bonehead and reached for the TV remote. "*Night Terrors* is about to come on."

"You know," Bonehead said, "I got to watch whatever I wanted while you were gone." He held the remote out of Stu's reach.

"Oh, yeah?" the wolf man said. "I hope you didn't get too used to it."

"I didn't," Bonehead replied with a shrug. "It made watching TV really boring."

"Yes," Beatrice agreed as she sank into a chair near the TV. "And there was no one here to frighten away the mailman while you were gone, Stu. Now I'm up to my neck in bills!"

"And I had no one to listen to my trumpet playing," Horror agreed.

"Are you saying that you missed me?" Wolf Man Stu asked. There was a lump in his throat.

"Let's just say that the Manor wasn't the same without you," Beatrice told him.

"Good," the werewolf said. He grinned and turned to Bonehead. "Now hand over the remote!"

"Make me!" Bonehead shouted, as he jumped off the couch, waving the remote in the air.

"I will!" Wolf Man Stu cried, as he leaped after Bonehead. Soon the two were tearing around the living room, shouting at the top of their lungs. Horror took out his trumpet, and put it to his lips. Instantly, the air filled with noise that sounded like a whoopee cushion with a bad case of the hiccups.

Professor Von Skalpel ran into the room, shouting, "Keep it down! Zome of us are trying to vork!"

"Be quiet, Professor!" Stu shouted. "Or I'll make a sandwich out of you! I'm a terrifying beast of the night, and you'd better not mess with me!"

"You already are a meth!" Bonehead said as he scurried under the table.

Stu raced after Bonehead, trying to hide his smile. I may be covered in itchy fur, he thought, and I may have fleas, but at least I'm back at the Manor.

With my friends.